DON'T ROCK THE ARK

Elizabeth Rodger

LILLIBETT BOOKS

For Avery

ISBN: 0-9839-2394-9   10 9 8 7 6 5 4 3 2 1

All was happy and peaceful in the animal world as the creatures went about their daily lives. Mrs. Elephant enjoyed the cool of a shower as Mr. Rhinoceros relished a mud bath and the lions rested in the shade.

The tallness of the Giraffes allowed them to see a distance. Mrs. Giraffe noticed movement on the horizon. A group of people was trudging toward them. "Strangers approaching," she called to Mr. Baboon, dozing on a branch.

"Wow! Strangers nearby! This has to be broadcast," announced Mr. Baboon. He rushed to tell Mr. Elephant for none was better spreading news when he raised his trunk and trumpeted far and wide.

Mr. Elephant agreed it was important news. He wasted no time raising his trunk and trumpeting, "Strangers in our midst." Such a commotion erupted as animals stopped their daily routines and rushed to hide.

A man called Noah led the strangers. He was accompanied by his wife, their sons, and their wives. As they continued on there was not an animal to be seen.

"We have frightened the animals and they are hiding," said Noah. He called to the animals. The gentleness of his voice reassured Mr. Elephant and he stepped from hiding. "Terrible rains will come and cause a great flood," explained Noah. "Follow us and we will save you."

Mr. Elephant threw up his trunk and trumpeted far and wide, "Don't be afraid. The strangers have come to save us."

Noah sent his family to the forests, fields, valleys, and mountains to collect two of every living creature. The animals came from hiding to meet them. Then, Noah led the animals on the long trek to safety.

After many days, the animals were tired and weary, but Noah gently urged them forward. They had to hurry for dark clouds were gathering. To Noah's relief, a huge ark came in sight. He and his sons had built the ark, and their wives had stored food inside for everyone.

Two by two, the animals hurried to enter the shelter of the ark.
Rain began to fall. Thunder boomed like great drums, and bolts of
lightning forked across the dark sky. Noah closed the door of the ark.
His family and two of every living creature were safe and dry inside.

Rain poured down harder and harder. Streams became rivers.
Rivers swelled until the water rushed over their banks and spread
across the land, covering fields and forest.

Suddenly, the ark was lifted by the rising water. It floated along gently as the water continued to rise, covering the hills and the mountains. Soon, the water covered all the land, and the ark floated on a great sea.

It was very crowded and very noisy inside the ark.

"I don't have enough room. Move over," Mrs. Crocodile snapped at Mr. Bear.

Mr. Bear jumped back and bumped into Mr. Rhinoceros who jabbed Mr. Elephant with his horn. Mr. Elephant stumbled backward and bumped Mrs. Elephant who staggered clumsily across the ark.

The ark began to roll wildly from side to side, and the air was filled with all kinds of screeching, howling, and roaring.

"Shh. Shh. Quiet, everyone. Please be still," Noah said. "Don't rock the ark," he pleaded.

Noah's gentle voice calmed the animals, and they soon settled back into their places.

The animals had to find a way to keep from rocking the ark. They all agreed the elephants shouldn't move. No sooner had they decided this than Mrs. Elephant let out a frightful shriek and reared back, her eyes rolling.

The ark began to tilt to one side.

"Please don't move, Mrs. Elephant," shouted Mr. Bear. "Don't rock the ark."

"That mouse ran over my toe," cried Mrs. Elephant, her big ears quivering with fright.

"Mrs. Mouse, you must stay away from Mrs. Elephant," scolded Mr. Bear. "Elephants are afraid of little mice like you."

"I'll try my best," said Mrs. Mouse, "but it's awfully crowded in here."

Just as the ark stopped rocking, a tiny flea came across a very thick and very wrinkled leg. The wrinkles made climbing quite easy.

"Oh, I have such an itch. I must scratch," roared Mr. Elephant. Mrs. Porcupine rushed to help. "Mr. Flea, you must get off his leg at once," she ordered. "You silly thing! We can't have Mr. Elephant scratching his leg. He'll rock the ark."

Mrs. Porcupine offered to scratch Mr. Elephant's leg
with her pointy quills. Then all was quiet again in the ark.

Mr. Peacock was sitting on a rafter where everyone could see and admire him. He fussed with and fluffed his beautiful feathers. He was a most handsome bird.

"Ah-aah," said Mrs. Elephant, her mouth opening wide. But she was not admiring Mr. Peacock. One of his bright green feathers had fallen on the end of Mrs. Elephant's long trunk, and it was tickling her terribly.

"Oh, no! She's going to sneeze," shouted a horrified Mr. Baboon. "We'll surely capsize if she does!" He leaped to the rescue.

With a puff of breath, Mr. Baboon blew the feather away. Then he held the end of Mrs. Elephant's trunk to stifle her sneeze. Aa-a-achoooo! It was a tiny sneeze for an elephant but it was strong enough to blow Mr. Baboon onto his back.

The animals settled down hoping their troubles with the Elephants were at an end. But all was not well.

"There isn't room to stretch my neck," said Mr. Giraffe.

"I'm so tired holding my head in the same position. My neck is quite stiff," complained Mrs. Giraffe.

"You poor things! You're welcome to rest your necks on my back," offered Mr. Elephant.

"That is very kind of you," said Mrs. Giraffe settling on a comfortable spot on his broad back. It didn't take long for the Giraffes to fall asleep.

When the Giraffes wakened from their nap, Mr. Elephant gave a long sad sigh.

"Is Mr. Flea bothering you again?" asked Mrs. Porcupine.

"No," replied Mr. Elephant. "It was an effort supporting the Giraffes' necks all the while standing in the same spot. I am so tired. I'll fall over if I don't lie down soon."

"Oh, no, you mustn't move," pleaded the animals. "You'll rock the ark if you do."

"Noah! Noah! Come quickly," Mr. Baboon called. "There's a disaster at hand."

When Noah heard about the problem, he thought hard for a moment. Then, he chuckled and clapped his hands together as he came up with a wonderful idea.

Noah took the thickest ropes he had and wove them into two huge hammocks. Then he hung them from the strongest of the wooden beams. The Elephants were delighted. They were so comfortable in the hammocks they dozed off immediately.

The other animals sighed with relief because the elephants could no longer rock the ark.

At last, all was peaceful.

One day, the animals felt a soft bump. Noah opened a window and saw that the ark had come to rest on the top of a mountain. The flood was drying up. As the water level dropped, land reappeared all around the ark.

Noah opened the door. Chattering and chirping happily, two by two, the Elephants, Giraffes, Kangaroos, Hippopotamuses, Bears, Rabbits, and all the animals hurried from the ark. Noah watched as they set off for the forests, fields, valleys, and mountains, to carry on with their lives.